AN ORIGIN STORY

Based on the Marvel comic book series The X-Men
Adapted by Rich Thomas
Interior Illustrated by The Storybook Art Group

New York

visit us at www.abdopublishing.com

Reinforced library bound edition published in 2013 by Spotlight, a division of the ABDO Group, PO Box 398166, Minneapolis, MN 55439. Spotlight produces high-quality reinforced library bound editions for schools and libraries. Published by agreement with Marvel Press, an imprint of Disney Book Group, LLC.

Printed in the United States of America, North Mankato, Minnesota.
042012
092012
♻ This book contains at least 10% recycled materials.

TM & © 2012 Marvel & Subs.

Cataloging-in-Publication Data

Thomas, Richard.
The uncanny x-men origin storybook / Adapted by Richard Thomas.
p. cm.
1. X-Men (Fictitious characters)—Juvenile fiction. 2. Superheroes—Juvenile ficton. 3. Good and evil—Juvenile fiction. I. Title.
PZ7.T36933 2012
[E]-dc223

ISBN 978-1-61479-012-9 (reinforced library edition)

All Spotlight books are reinforced library binding and manufactured in the United States of America.

Did you ever have a dream that felt so real,

that you were sure you weren't **dreaming** at all?

This is a story about a boy named
CHARLES XAVIER who dreamed
he could do many things that an
ordinary boy could not.

He dreamed his mind could leave his body and float like a feather.

He dreamed he could know what other people were **thinking** before they even opened their mouths to speak.

But Charles didn't want to tell other people about his special dreams, because he was afraid of how they would treat him.

So Charles dreamed of a world where people like himself—people who felt different—could be proud to be themselves.

But those dreams would always end abruptly.

You see, the world didn't seem like a very fair place to Charles. His father had passed away when he was just a young boy.

He lived in his father's mansion with his mother, who loved him very much.

But his older brother and his stepfather lived in the mansion, too. And they were **heartless** and **cruel** to Charles and his mother.

Charles didn't look like other kids, either.

He began to lose his hair at a very young age. And by the time he was a teenager, Charles's head was completely bare.

But that was not all.

Charles had always heard whispers of things that no one was saying out loud. As he grew older, he began to hear them more and more clearly. Eventually Charles realized that he could read minds.

As time went by and Charles grew older,
he used his gift to gain knowledge.

He studied to become a doctor of science. He wanted to
learn more about why he had these special powers.

Charles soon discovered that he was a mutant—a person born with special abilities.

His studies took him all over the world. And while in Egypt, Charles met another mutant for the first time.

This mutant was evil, and Charles had to stop him. So they fought on the astral plane. And Charles won.

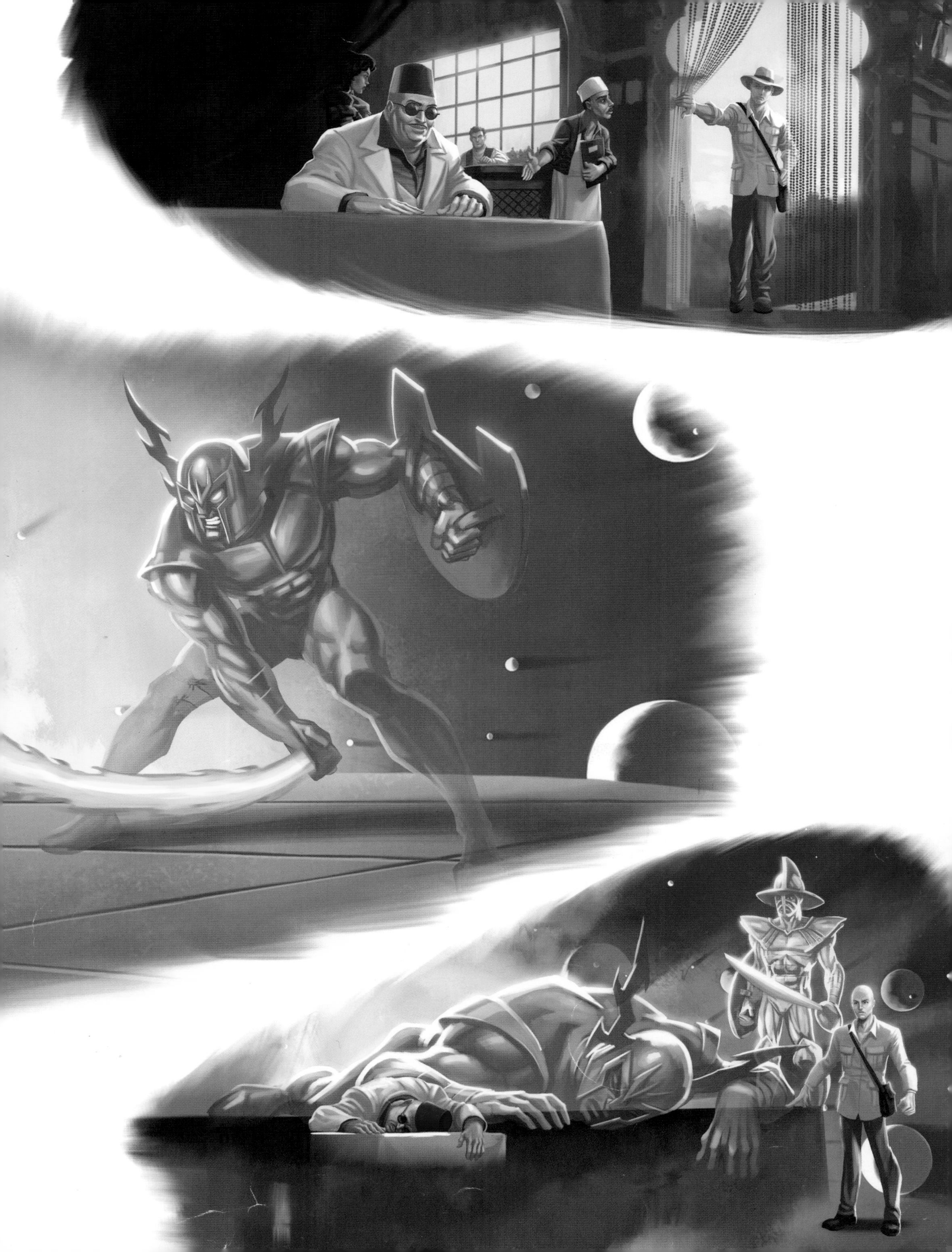

Charles soon met another mutant—a man named **ERIK MAGNUS**.

Magnus had the mutant power to move metal objects without touching them. Charles and Magnus became fast friends. But they did not always agree.

Magnus knew humans feared and hated mutants. He thought the only way for mutants to keep themselves safe was to use their powers to take over the world.

But Charles still dreamed of a world where humans and mutants could live together peacefully.

Charles and Magnus met and defeated an evil human named
BARON VON STRUCKER who wanted to use his wealth to destroy
anyone he didn't like.

Magnus felt that this
proved humans were bad.
He took the Baron's gold
and flew away with it,
telling Charles he was
foolish to believe that
mankind was good.

Charles was sad to lose his friend. As he continued his travels, he began to think about **returning home**.

But during a stop on his journey, Charles encountered an alien named **Lucifer**. He wanted to destroy both humans **and** mutants.

They fought, and the alien brought down his secret hideaway on top of Charles. Charles survived, but his legs had been crushed. He would never again be able to walk.

He returned home, more determined than ever to find other mutants. He would train them to fight any threat—mutant, human, or alien.

Charles's mother and stepfather had passed away, and his brother had left the mansion long ago. The Xavier home was empty, but it wouldn't stay that way for long.

The first mutant Charles
found was named **SCOTT
SUMMERS**. Charles called
him Cyclops for the optic
blasts he could shoot from
his eyes.

Next, Charles and Cyclops
rescued a teenager from an
angry mutant-hating mob.
The boy, **BOBBY DRAKE**,
could turn himself into ice
and called himself Iceman.

Then the growing group found **WARREN WARTHINGTON III**, who called himself Angel for the wings that helped him fly.

And finally **HANK MCCOY** joined the team. Hank was called The Beast because of his large hands and feet, which helped him swing like a monkey and punch like a gorilla.

Charles renamed the mansion **Xavier's School for Gifted Youngsters**. To the outside world, it was just another boarding school. But secretly, it was a school for young mutants to learn how to use their powers. The students were given uniforms, and each pledged to fight for Charles's dream.

Charles called himself **Professor X** and his team the **X-Men**, because each member had an extraordinary power.

The X-Men soon welcomed their fifth and final founding member— **JEAN GREY**, called **Marvel Girl**. Jean could move things with her mind.

Professor X then built a computer to locate other mutants. The machine, called **Cerebro**, showed that a mutant was attacking an army base.

It was the
Professor's
old friend Magnus!

Now known as **Magneto**, he had used the baron's gold to wage war on the human race.

Charles knew that only the **X-Men** could stop his old friend!

The X-Men arrived at the base just
as Magneto began to attack.

And so the **X-Men** sprang into action and attacked him right back.

Cyclops tried to blast through Magneto's magnetic field. But he couldn't.

Magneto guided every missile that Marvel Girl tried to send at him right back at her.

Angel and The Beast did not fare much better.

At last, Magneto attacked them all. But Marvel Girl covered her teammates with a force field.

The X-Men were not so easily defeated!

The X-Men had come to stop Magneto and turn him over to the police. But Magneto had escaped.

The X-Men were disappointed. But Professor X told them he was very proud of them for stopping the attack.

Over the next few months, the X-Men trained in a special gym called the Danger Room. The room was filled with obstacles to help the X-Men perfect their abilities.

And Professor X used Cerebro to keep a constant watch for new mutants.

And he found many! But more often than not, the mutants were evil.

After many battles, the X-Men graduated and became full-fledged heroes. Professor X had never been prouder of his students.

He retired their school uniforms and dressed them in new costumes. But the end of their school days did not mean the end of their missions. In fact, things only got more difficult for the X-Men.

More mutants were appearing each day, and humans were becoming more and more concerned. They were afraid of the mutants's powers. Even though the X-Men tried to protect humans and live Professor Xavier's dream, people treated **all** mutants badly.

As mutants grew in number, so did the X-Men. Cyclops's brother Alex Summers—an energy-blasting mutant called Havok—and Lorna Dane, called Polaris for her magnetic abilities, joined the team.

But their group was still too small to fight all of the threats. And when the X-Men went missing on a dangerous mission, Professor X had to assemble a new group to rescue them.

Toronto   Dublin   Moscow
Berlin

Nairobi

In Canada, he recruited a mutant named **Wolverine** who could heal himself of any injury and whose claws could cut through almost anything!

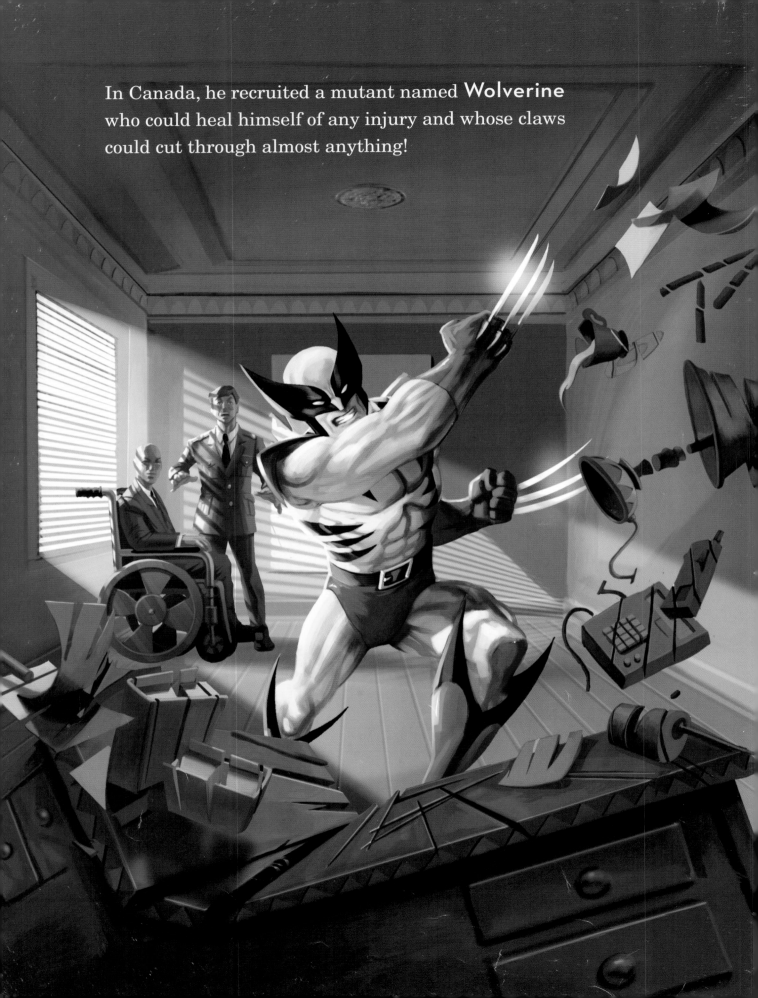

In Germany, Charles found **KURT WAGNER**, called Nightcrawler, who could move from place to place with just a thought.

Together with Wolverine and Nightcrawler, Professor X decided to seek out more good mutants to help rescue the original X-Men.

In Ireland, Charles found **SEAN CASSIDY**—Banshee—whose sonic scream could shatter stone and steel.

In Africa, Charles met **ORORO MUNROE**, a weather mutant called Storm.

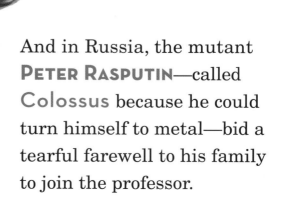

And in Russia, the mutant **PETER RASPUTIN**—called Colossus because he could turn himself to metal—bid a tearful farewell to his family to join the professor.

Charles's new international team wasted no time
in their search to find the Original X-Men.

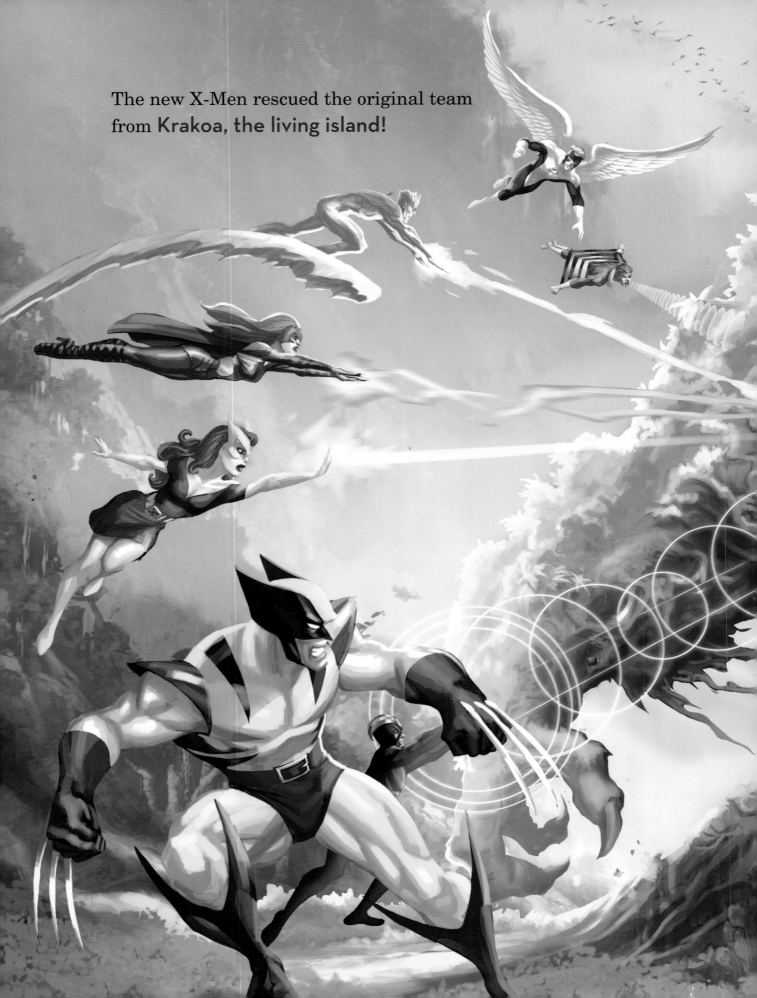

The new X-Men rescued the original team from **Krakoa**, the living island!

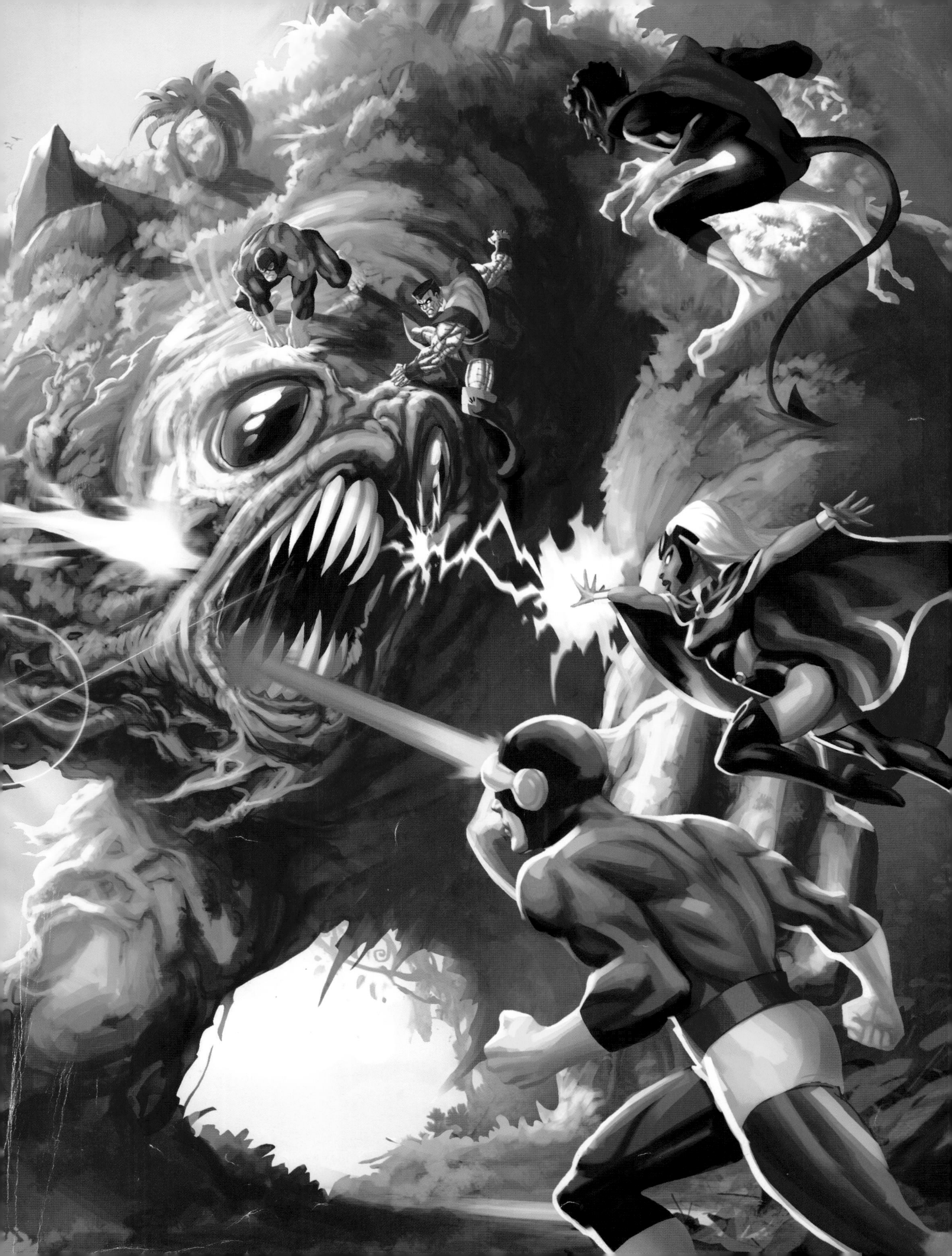

The new group decided to stay at
Xavier's school.

They trained to use their powers.
Soon they too became X-Men.

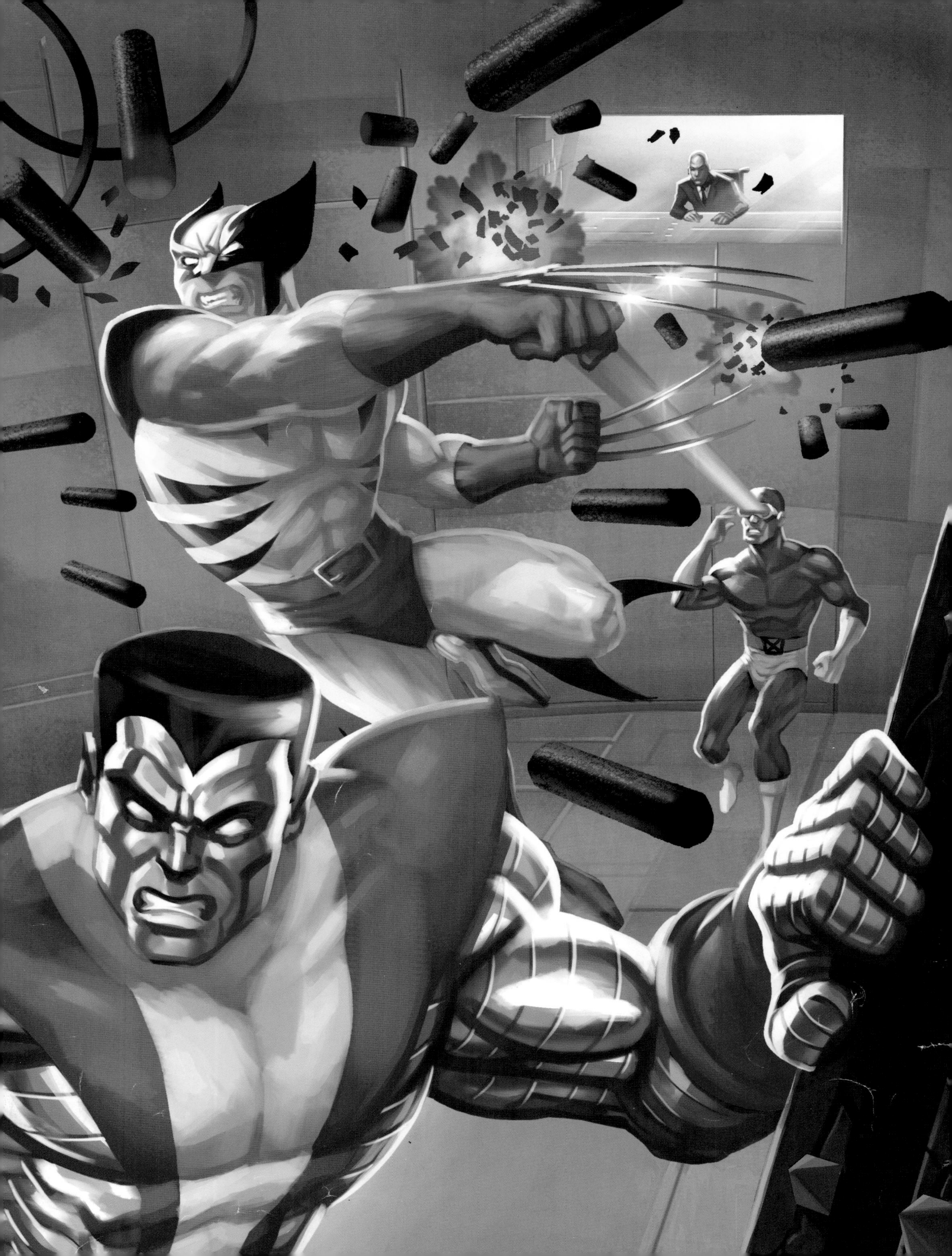

They were a kind of family. But no matter what the X-Men did . . .

. . . trouble seemed to find them.

No matter the day, month, or season . . .

. . . the X-Men were
never safe.

Enemies both **old** and **new** were always attacking.

And with every incident, humans
became more worried about mutants.

But with every battle, **Charles** felt the
need to fight harder for his dream.

And whenever Charles felt hope leaving him,

he'd lie down, just as he did when he was a boy,

close his eyes, drift off to sleep . . .

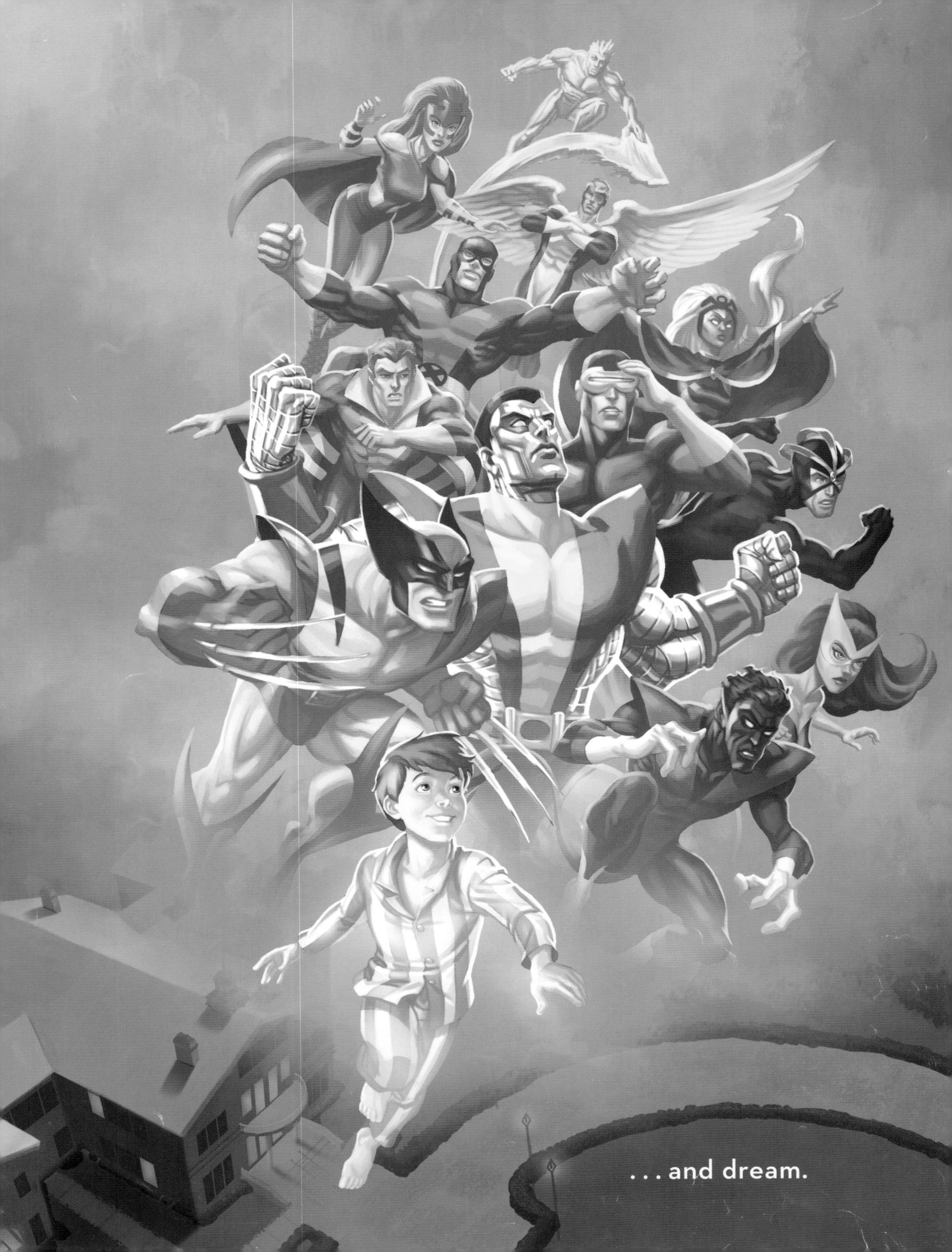
. . . and dream.